Where's Ted?

Colin and
Jacqui Hawkins

ORCHARD BOOKS

This is Harry!

This is
Harry's mum.

This is
Harry's dad . . .

. . . and Harry's
big brother, Tom.

This is
Harry's granny,

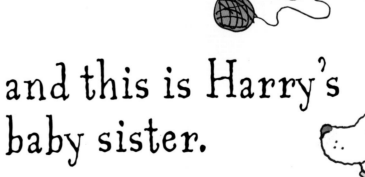

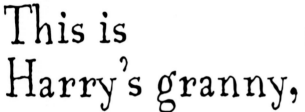

and this is Harry's
baby sister.

Here is Pip, the dog! But . . .

...where is Harry's teddy bear?

Harry looked in his toy box
and found . . .

Is Ted in Mum's handbag?

Mum looked in her handbag
and Harry found . . .

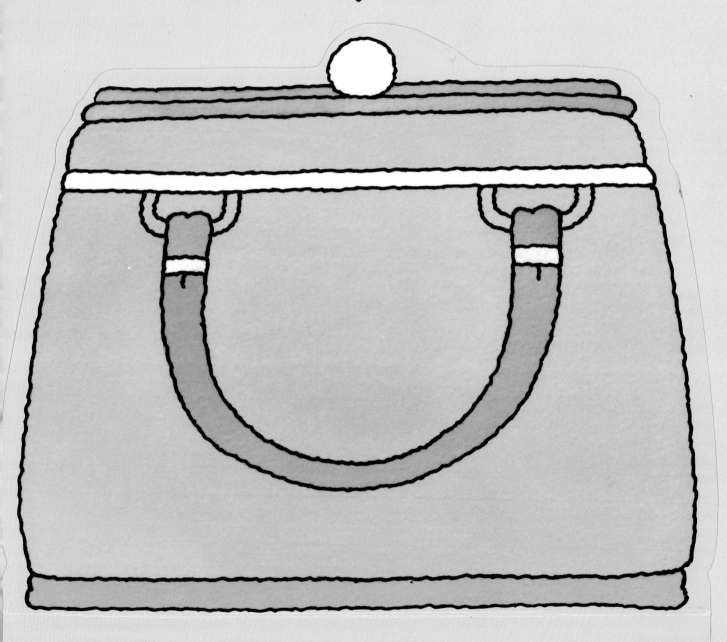

Is Ted in Dad's tool box?

Dad looked in his tool box
and Harry found . . .

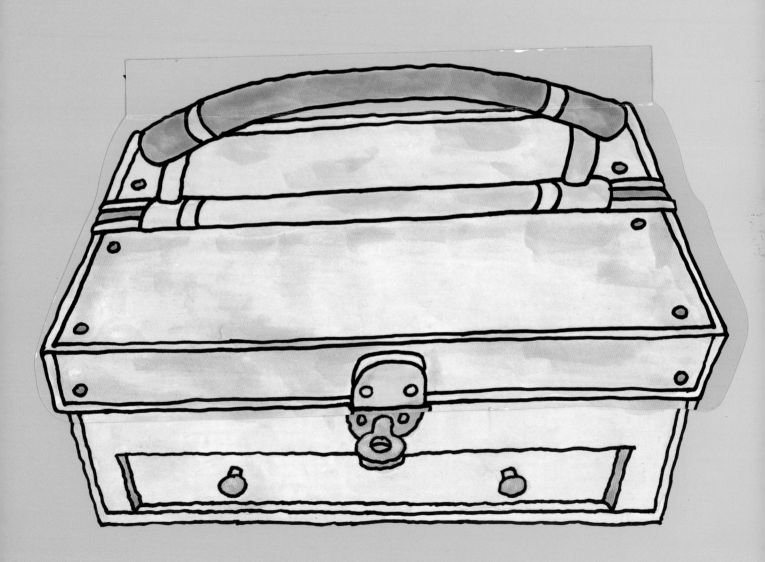

Could Ted be in Granny's big bag?

Granny looked in her big bag
and Harry found . . .

Perhaps Ted is in Tom's school bag?

Tom looked in his school bag
and Harry found . . .

Is Ted in Baby Bear's bag?

Harry looked in Baby Bear's
bag and found . . .

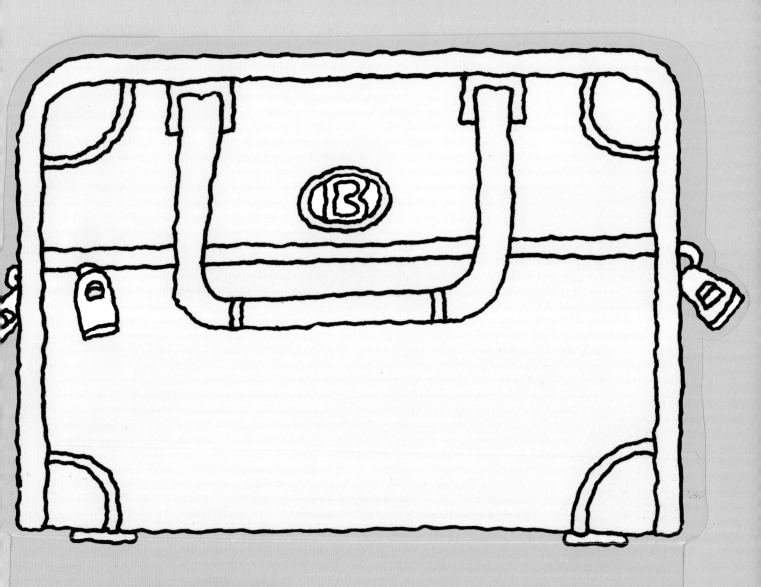

Harry had looked everywhere for Ted.

He'd looked
in his toy box,

in Mum's
handbag

and in Dad's
tool box.

He'd looked in
Granny's
big bag,

and Big Brother
Tom's school bag.

And even in
Baby Bear's bag.

He had looked everywhere except . . .

...in Pip's basket!
Could Ted be there?

Harry looked in Pip's basket
and he found . . .

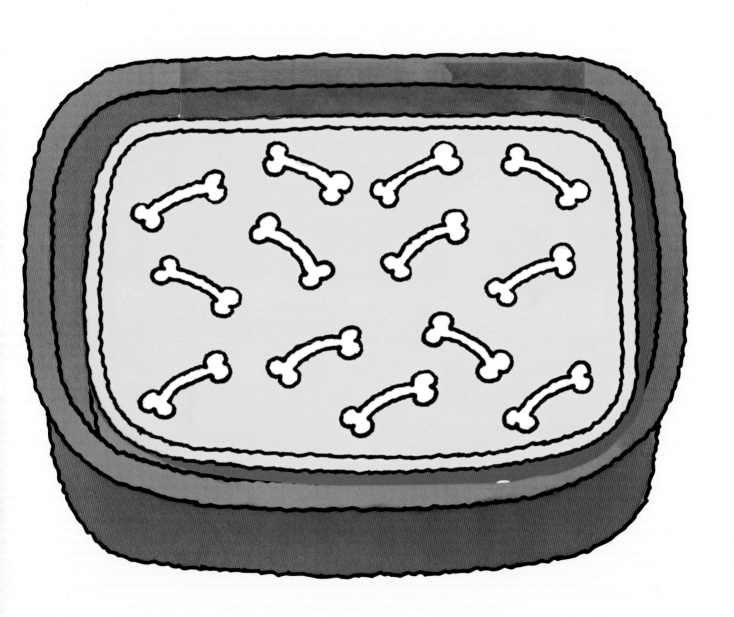

Later Pip couldn't find
Harry or Ted.

Where could they be?